SOLOMON SACKITEY

# ROADMAP

This study guide is based on the book, *Circumstances* by the same author.
The characters, organizations, locations, names, businesses, institutions,
incidents, events, among others portrayed, are fictitious or used fictitiously.
Any similarity to locales, events, real locations or real individuals (living
or not), is entirely coincidental and or used to illustrate educational and or
cultural awareness.

The goal of this book is to provide roadmaps to the concepts, episodes, and
various terminologies, for example, for a good understanding and educational
entertainment or edutainment of *Circumstances*.

Disclaimer: Among other things, this study guide is not intended to provide
medical advice, diagnosis, treatment or any professional advice related to any
and or other industries or sectors in any way. Products and literature cited are
for educational purposes only and do not necessarily reflect any and all forms
of approval, integrity or endorsement. All website addresses provided are for
further reading and knowledge enhancement purposes. There is no conflict of
interest whatsoever with reference to the copyright owners of listed websites
and other resources. Citing these weblinks is not an endorsement, approval,
validation of integrity, support, or the like whatsoever. There is no guarantee
that website links listed will last indefinitely. Readers are advised to do their
own research or due diligence pertaining to the subject matter of interest
should the links become nonfunctional or have any issues. In addition,
patrons of these websites are advised to address concerns with the copyright
owners directly.

Christian and Muslim references made in this study guide or in
*Circumstances* are not intended to disrespect or disregard any and or all
other religions or religious and non-religious beliefs.

Biblical verses referenced in this story are not direct quotations from any
particular version of the Bible but synopses that could be found in various
versions of the Words of God (The Bible).

Discretion: This book may contain material(s) or scenarios that may not be
appropriate for everybody. Discretionary decision-making is advised.

# DEDICATION

**This book is dedicated to my:**

**Lovely children,**
for their motivation and continuous encouragements.

**Belated parents and stepmothers,**
who gave all they could to hold together a large but loving and closely-knit family.

**Colleague and friend, Mr. Philip S. Stinard,**
who passed away prior to the final preparation of this book. He was a superior geneticist, motivator and teacher that will be missed for generations.

**Siblings,**
who were major forces that supported my parents and stepmothers.

**Exceptional mentors, friends, loved ones and well-wishers,**
for being the unknown heroes.

**In addition, the book is dedicated to:**

**The late Mr. S. Kwansa and his wife,**
who paved the way for the genesis of the realization of some of my dreams.

**Dr. and Dr. (Mrs.) S. Okiror,**
who made some of my dreams come true and for proving that dreams can come true.

**Sylvie Mallet,**
for her solid support and prayers besides inculcating the belief that faith can overshadow intimidation and obstacles.

# ACKNOWLEDGEMENT

Philip S. Stinard of blessed memory. Mr. Philip Stinard is greatly and sincerely appreciated. In the midst of other time-sensitive deadlines, he made relentless efforts to review this manuscript. He also provided suggestions not of miniature values but of tremendous imaginations. May his soul rest in eternal peace.

## ABOUT THE BOOK

In stimulating and attracting a wide range of perspectives on episodes, themes and other sections of the thought-provoking short story entitled *Circumstances,* this study guide or roadmap has been constructed. It explains basic terminologies, provides the reader a good ground for discussions and wets the appetite for travels to places of special interest that you may want to see for yourself before you pass away. In addition, this book explains selected episodes, chants, and objects while it throws in some questions to illuminate a number of debates.

The roadmap helps in tracing the coming-of-age journey of the main character.

# ABOUT THE AUTHOR

An Adjunct Lecturer in Regulatory Affairs for Drugs, Biologics and Medical Devices courses at one of the most prestigious universities in the United States (US), Solomon Sackitey is also an Editorial Board member of an International Medical Science Journal in America. He earned a Bachelor's degree in Biochemistry and a Master's degree in pharmaceutical Regulatory Affairs at Iowa State University and Northeastern University, respectively. Solomon's broad background and experience embrace serving as a Research Scientist engaged in HIV DNA Vaccines Research and Development. In addition, he served as a Laboratory Logistics Director involved in coordinating swine flu clinical specimen testing in collaboration with the World Health Organization/U.S. Centers for Disease Control and Prevention. He also worked as a Senior Regulatory Affairs Specialist. A teacher, learner, and loving family man, he is a passionate volunteer with a United Nations Volunteer-of-The-Year Award to his credit. Solomon has two United States patents and has authored and/or co-authored several scientific and public health articles. He is the author of three books: *A Sea of Plight* and *Pure Joy of The GOLD COAST BOY* (under the pen name, Bwana Awetse), *Circumstances,* and *Roadmap.* As a contributing author, he wrote for the PRESEC-Legon School Magazine, *Iowa Agriculturalist* and the *Iowa State Daily.* His three undergraduate research findings were published in the Maize Genetics Cooperation Newsletter.

# CONTENTS

Glossary ........................................................................... 1

The Plot Landscape ........................................................ 7

Main Character Sketches ............................................... 11

Understanding Selected Themes, Motifs, and Objects .......... 17

Selected Episode Scrutiny ............................................. 25

Analysis of Selected Quotations ..................................... 33

Interpretation of The Afadjato Chant ............................. 39

Selected Fiction and Nonfiction ..................................... 41

Study Questions and Discussions .................................... 47

Suggested Further Readings and Selected Trails in the
Gold Coast Boy Expedition ............................................ 57

Acknowledgement ........................................................ 73

# GLOSSARY

**Biotechnology:** Biotechnology is a multidisciplinary field including biological sciences, computer information technology, and engineering. Using DNA technology and other technologies, it describes a modern approach to addressing issues in medicine, health systems, food science, nutrition, and the environment, for the rapid sustainable developments in scientific research, technology, safety and regulations.

**Chimeric:** Outside of the popular biological sciences definition and per the Dictionary, Chimeric means, "(of a mythical animal) formed from parts of various animals." For example, "the design is based on a chimeric creature with the body of a turtle and the head of a dragon." Retrieved on April 10, 2018 from https://www.dictionary.com/browse/chimeric

**CRISPR**. CRISPR stands for **C**lustered **R**egularly **I**nterspaced **S**hort **P**alindromic **R**epeats. It is a promising biotechnology tool for editing the genome of a number of organisms for many medical and nonmedical considerations. Cas9 which is the CRISPR-associated protein 9 can be used in a variety of techniques for gene editing and elucidating epigenetics, among others.

More information on genome editing and CRISPR can be accessed at https://ghr.nlm.nih.gov/primer/genomicresearch/genomeediting. Retrieved on May 8, 2019.

**"Cultural intelligence (CQ)** is the capability to relate and work effectively in culturally diverse situations. It goes beyond existing notions of cultural sensitivity and awareness to highlight a theoretically-based set of capabilities needed to successfully and respectively accomplish your objectives in culturally diverse settings". Retrieved from https://culturalq.com/what-is-cq/ on 10th September, 2018.

**Culture:** Outside of biology, culture is neither about the difference between a British and a Japanese nor the difference between an American and an African, for example.

**Discrimination**: the unjust treatment or biased consideration of people or things based on several factors including, but not limited to, physical disability or ability, sexual orientation, gender, skin color, race, tribal affiliation, educational, social, economic, national origin or religious affiliation.

**Epigenetics:** Genetic inheritance without a change in the DNA sequence or codons.

**Genetic Engineering:** The manipulation of the deoxyribonucleic acid (DNA) molecule or the building blocks (nucleotides) of DNA to yield various biological products and processes.

**Genetically Modified:** When an organism's DNA alphabets (nucleotides) are altered in a number of ways, they are said to be genetically modified.

**GMO:** This is the abbreviated version of Genetically Modified Organism. GMO is a technology that uses a multitude of tools in the biological sciences, computer technology, physical sciences, for example, to change, or enhance traits and/or properties of living things like plants, animals, medicines, an so on. This terminology has been made popular due to advances in deoxyribonucleic acid technology (DNA technology). Some people interchangeably refer to GMO as biotechnology, genetic engineering or bioengineering, for instance.

**Omnipotent:** Most powerful, supreme, unlimited power.

**Opulent:** magnificent, splendid, gorgeous, beautiful.

**Resilience:** the courage and ability to get back up and chase your dreams after meeting or encountering challenges, difficulties or setbacks in life (e.g. in sports, school, at the work place or personal relationships). [Can you think of another way of defining resilience in your own words? Can you describe one or two circumstances where you or your friends demonstrated or showed resilience?].

**Tenacity:** the continued self-determination or motivation to succeed no matter how tough the circumstances may be. This "yes, I can" quality in an individual can yield many fruits from laboring.

# THE PLOT LANDSCAPE

The plot landscape includes the author as a main character and story-teller.

The plot centers around a young boy from the small African town of Asesewa in the Eastern Region of Ghana which is well known for its market, The Asesewa Market (now glorified as the Asesewa Mall or the Asesewa Rural Mall). The Asesewa Market magnetizes merchants to the town on Fridays and Mondays.

The plot traces the paths or the trajectories of steep, winding expeditions for decades. Along these paths come life-changing tornadoes, torpedoes, volcanoes, resurrected dodoes, blazing heat waves and honey all backed by faith and God's guidance.

The author himself plays a main character role along a titillating array of brilliant episodes epitomized by The Gold Coast Boy (GCB), Mr. and Mrs. Oleman (Gold Coast Boy's parents), Teye, Mercy, Ama, Ms. Abbosey, Nina, TJ, Abigail (Tsetse Fly), Abiba, and Dubious Fraudsters, to mention a few.

# MAIN CHARACTER SKETCHES

**A.** Gold Coast Boy. A young and ambitious gentleman now in his forties who has come of age, Gold Coast Boy is a five-foot six inches (1.68 meters) chap that does not dwell on his past or let any challenges stop him from moving forward. His belief in the omen enshrined in the Afadjato chant carried through generations of the Oleman clan, firmly backed by faith in God, propels him to new heights when everything seems to turn against him. He is a free-willed guy and not self-centered. He is usually seen with dreadlocks or Rastaman hair style. Gold Coast Boy's preferred clothing is a red pair of shorts and gold T-shirt with Adidas tennis shoes. His physique is characterized by very muscular upper body, thick hips and strong legs that most athletes' can boast of.

The author serves as the protagonist and Gold Coast Boy.

**B.** IBM (Ibrahim Mahamadose); Ibrahim. The potential "Lost-and-To-Be-Found" friend of Gold Coast Boy, now in his forties also, is six-foot six inches (1.98 meters) tall (based on family traits and composite pictures), an agile man with very light skin complexion, curly brown hair, thick black eye brows, a pointed nose, and a fore-head the shape of a coconut fruit. He weighs in at one hundred and ninety-eight pounds (ninety kilograms).

**C.** Mercy. A no-nonsense girl, Mercy and Teye are at loggerheads most of the time; yet, they are the best of friends as they are seen hanging out together everytime. You can hardly see Mercy without Teye. Mercy is a devout feminist. The 5 feet 8 inches (1.73 meters) girl with athletic features is full of self-confidence and brags about her high level of intelligence. Mercy is very industrious and eloquent.

**D.** Teye He is 4 feet 4 inches (1.32 meters) tall, big mouthed, opinionated; yet, funny. Sadly, Teye believes that boys are superior to girls. He learns the hard way that his views are foolish and not funny. A younger brother of the Gold Coast Boy, Teye is very talkative and argumentative. Nicknamed, The Lawyer, he is the smallest person in the story who can brainstorm events. Teye is seen mostly wearing a pair of black shorts, green T-shirt with only one sleeve, putting on a pair of sandals on the wrong foot. He wears a white baseball hat backwards. His insatiable craving for sweets and fatty foods makes him overweight. Teye is a very intelligent guy who enjoys reading and sketching people's characters.

**E.** Abigail (Tsetse Fly). Abigail is so sneaky. In fact, her character is so similar to that of the tsetse fly, a blood sucking insect which can cause the trypanosomiasis disease or sleeping sickness in humans and animals. Putting it in real perspectives, Abigail is good at swindling people of their money to the extent of getting them dead broke. Her relatively long and protruding nose which she uses to sniff potentially wealthy targets matches that of the tsetse fly.

**F.** Mrs. Oleman is a family-oriented housewife who is enriched with wisdom, peace and tranquility. A Christian, Mrs. Oleman always reads the Bible with her children and the family as a whole.

**G.** Oleman is the stalwart of the family and the Oleman clan. He is an ethical disciplinarian. His strength is in raising the family based on the principles and teachings of the Christian literature. He is never seen angry or abusive. He lays a lot of emphasis on education as he strongly believes that education can eradicate poverty, hunger and malnutrition. He encourages his children to seek knowledge by travelling because travelling by itself is education.

**H.** Nina Willie. When it comes to making people happy and forgetting about their problems in life, nobody beats Nina Willie. She is very influential, endowed with philanthropy and wisdom. She can put smiles on the faces of people all the time. Her weakness is that she is a chain smoker who smokes several packs of cigarettes a day and never eats her lunch and dinner without her bottles of wine and whisky, respectively.

**I.** Abiba, in some ways, is like Abigail. She thrives in coordinating fraudulent activities and uses her position in mass media communication to attract vulnerable victims. She is well educated and has travelled to over 25 countries in Africa, Europe, Asia, North America, The Caribbean, Australia, Mexico and Argentina---basically, around the world on business trips.

**J.** Tom Jayson (TJ) is a traitor. All his mission is to take advantage of his friends who confide in him. It does not matter to him how long he has been friends to anyone or how much a friend sacrifices to come to his aid.

# NOTES

# UNDERSTANDING SELECTED THEMES, MOTIFS, AND OBJECTS

**A.** The "invention" of Chimeric is a rare mythical "creature" based on the genetic modification of the bamboo tree, baobab tree, and the amphibious chimeric animals comprising a donkey-turtle, a cheetah-lion, a hawk-dragon and a horse-giraffe.

The bamboo tree symbolizes strength; it is used heavily to fortify the creation of Chimeric and provides protection against hurricanes, monsoons, typhoons, and potential attacks of whales, or similar natural disasters.

Moreover, the bamboo tree shows the tensile strength needed to overcome all unforeseeable dangers in the path to accomplishing a mission.

The baobab tree is used as an emblem of longevity, durability and good health.

The *amphibious chimeric donkey-turtle* depicts the fact that even though some dreams may be slow to accomplish, they are indeed, within reach.

The *amphibious cheetah-lion chimeric* creature, combines the supersonic speeds of the speedster animals with the speed of light; thus enabling Chimeric to fly high. This creature also symbolizes that some dreams can be achieved very rapidly.

The *amphibious horse-giraffe-zebra* chimeric also is used here to convey the notion of rigidity, toughness, and resilience when one pursues dreams. At the same time, this creation is used to demonstrate what it takes to fly in a challenging weather and operate undersea or land when hopes of overcoming major obstacles are almost zero.

When it comes to shooting high for the skies or following your dreams, the *amphibious hawk-dragon chimeric* creature is one you can count on.

In effect, the creation of Chimeric is a fable with the embodiment of a donkey-turtle, a cheetah-lion, a horse-giraffe-zebra, and a hawk-dragon. In addition to the bamboo and baobab trees, sensors or forces, these components of Chimeric make it act as characters endowed with the power to withstand natural disasters and attacks by omnivores in the ocean, rainforests, deserts, savannas, not to mention carnivores and herbivores.

Chimeric biosubmarine creates a world of Innovation taking into consideration the catastrophes, challenges, complexities and opportunities of the past, present and the future. It also traces the influence of religious beliefs and ethics on modern day biotechnology.

The interior of Chimeric is equipped with security cameras, a kitchen, sports arena, and remote sensing devices including GPS (Global Positioning Systems) that identify objects including human beings, goats, antelopes, and deers at any time, day, or night.

It can take pictures and store them in the Chimeric Cloud Database (CCD), Blockchain or Artificial Intelligence (AI) data transmissible worldwide.

Gold Cost Boy can access and control this device remotely. The GPS is functional whether Chimeric is stalled, stationary or operational.

**B.** The bamboo tree is a plant known for its longevity and stellar strength. In the story, Ama equates Gold Coast Boy's strength to that of the bamboo tree. She enjoys calling him the bamboo man.

**C.** A baobab tree is a giant perennial tree of life known for its longevity that spans decades of fruitful life. Ama and Gold Coast Boy's marriage is blessed to last as long as the baobab tree. In real life, the baobab tree on the former campus of the Presbyterian Boys' Secondary School (PRESEC) at Odumase-Krobo in Ghana lasted for at least fifty years before passing on to eternity.

**D.** In the globalized economy, culture cannot be taken for granted. There is a price to pay for not being conversant with cultural intelligence. Gold Coast Boy and his convoy learn the hard way the importance of culture in Nigeria. It is imperative to be sensitive and aware of cultural, ethnic and religious diversity, among others.

**E.** Corn detasseling is portrayed in this story to show that hard work pays off. It also indicates that there is no such thing as a dirty job.

**F.** Sports. Ama and her soccer drills bring to the forefront women's excellence in sports or in changing the world for the better. The myth that boys are better than girls does not hold water.

**G.** Thieves, fraudsters and scammers. These teach the reader and the listener to be on the lookout every time because anyone can be a victim at any time in any given location.

**H.** Friendship can be demonstrated in many ways through athletics as seen in the Drake Relays. Friendliness and kindness can travel a long way and turn around like a boomerang. Be kind and friendly with no strings attached.

**I.** Unethical politics and the lack of humility destroy society and the future. They can lead to harming innocent children, the youth and future leadership. The tumultuous and adrenalizing journeys of Gold Coast Boy would not have happened if it is not for the absence of ethical politics. Self-aggrandizement and humungous egos exhibited in politics can be stumbling blocks in the path of innovation.

**J.** Geography. Throughout the story, geography is prominently displayed. Knowledge about geography can promote travel, tourism, and global events.

**K.** History builds the case for learning lessons from the past and the present while we write the history of yesterday, today, and tomorrow. It can include immigration issues and political instability.

**L.** Optimism, perseverance and self-confidence along with being one another's keeper are vital in overcoming obstacles in life as we read in the story.

**M.** Communication, rhetoric and the ability to speak another person's language can alleviate several problems and pave the way to accomplishing several goals in life. At the same time, the reader and the listener are cautioned about the mischiefs of others who can use their God-given gift of rhetory to cause havoc or distractions as we read in several instances in this story.

NOTES

# NOTES

# SELECTED EPISODE SCRUTINY

**1.** Family drama and the Theology of Genetic Engineering in Ghana prior to the commencement of Gold Coast Boy's second journey.

We learn in this episode about family values, basic knowledge of genetics and the future—yesterday, today and tomorrow. It is important to stay connected not only with the nucleus family but also with the extended family and friends. With this in mind, Gold Coast Boy seeks the blessings from his enlarged family before he travels.

This section also deals with following dreams. The dreams could be to seek further academic knowledge, pursuing business ventures or entrepreneurial prospects, travelling in search of something or somebody special; whatever you want to accomplish in this world within a limited time. Not dwelling on the past, staying tuned to events in contemporary times and not being afraid to stick your neck into the future define the path(s) to accomplishing your dream(s).

The future of medicine, family genetic identity, challenges and benefits of biotechnology have been explored in funny scenarios highlighted by Teye, Mercy, Mr. and Mrs. Oleman besides Gold Coast Boy himself who is also the author. Be sure to identify when he acts as the Gold Coast Boy or when it is the author speaking or acting.

**2.** Following dreams does not come easily or in a short duration for many people. The second voyage to Nigeria is marked by lamentations as well as revelation of God's interventions. Gold Coast Boy is caught in a gunpoint episode in the midst of military-university student confrontation although he was not a university student in Nigeria. In this real life event, several students from Nigeria and foreign countries get killed during the student riots but God intervened in poor Gold Coast Boy's case and his life gets saved.

What happens when Gold Coast Boy seeks medical attention during his beating by the Nigerian military brings up one major problem in society--Corruption.

In an environment where corruption reigns, various strategies are employed to find ways and means for by-passing children and pregnant women who spend almost the entire day in queues and lying down on pieces of cloth spread on the floor in order to get treatment for Gold Coast Boy and other patients.

**3.** Betrayal of friendship. TJ and Abigail, hungry for money and power, do everything to virtually rob and betray a good old friend and classmate of Gold Coast Boy. It is important to know that people do change. A friend at one point in time becomes a traitor at another time. Be careful. This section makes everyone wonder if it is really worth risking Gold Coast Boy's life searching for his childhood friend, Ibrahim. What if he does not cherish or value their childhood friendship after so many years of not being in touch? What if Ibrahim does not care about Gold Coast Boy the way he used to?

**4.** False leads. For the most part in a world of fraud, Gold Coast Boy encounters many instances where he is faced with swindlers and jokers including, but not limited to, Abiba, Le Garcon and Andy.

**5.** The visit to an unknown Island symbolizes a world of friendliness, peace and harmony. Gold Coast Boy gets welcomed by the Islands' inhabitants who have no clue whom he is, what his motives are for visiting the Islands and unable to speak the Island's language nor do their hawk dance. Gold Coast Boy could have been held a hostage and taken to be terrorist or a spy. And the world would have never known about his whereabouts. Sheila comes to Gold Coast Boy's rescue as a Certified Translator of the Hawk Language.

**6.** Undersea mission. Travel, hunting and survival. This episode is carried out to make sure there is no stone unturned in the search for Ibrahim. Guess what you may find under the stone? Your guess is as good as mine.

Retrieved on March 6, 2019 from https://www.google.com/search?q=Undersea+travels+and+undersea+hunting&client=ms-android-att-us&prmd=insv&source=lnms&tbm=isch&sa=X&ved=2ahUKEwjum8yT8cjgAhVGtlkKHQrzDE4Q_AUoAXoECAwQAQ&biw=360&bih=560

**7.** The WAM entertainers. The London episode demonstrates that life is not full of darkness. Nina and her WAM Group do everything to make GCB and his Nigerian colleagues feel at home. The WAM Group appears to be peachy. Soft on the outside. Hopefully so on the inside.

**8.** The corn detasseling rescue. Manny KojoKutu comes to the aid on the stranded vanpool crew during the aftermaths of the collision with a deer which results in a deflated tire. At the same time, Gold Coast Boy makes some discoveries about Ibrahim which get him really confused based on apparently true stories of two friends, Andy and Niifio.

**9.** True friendship. *The Drake Relays* redefines what true friendship is. It also spells out what it takes to follow one's dreams: resilience, faith and help along the way. What Gold Coast Boy and Ibrahim portrayed is indicative of not giving up. It builds the case for unity, and by being each other's keeper, the world will continue to revolve on its axis.

**10.** The magic of speaking the other person's language. When Gold Coast Boy speaks French in France and at the wedding reception in Tanzania, there is magic, so to speak. He sparks excitement at the wedding while he is left off the hook in Paris.

**11.** Unethical politics. Wow, what politics can do to society is unpredictable. What it does to humanity in various cases including immigration issues and the national or global economy can be disastrous in several people's journeys to fulfil their lifetime dreams especially when unethical political strategies are devised or implemented.

NOTES

NOTES

# ANALYSIS OF SELECTED QUOTATIONS

**1.** Oleman: "All these are against the powers of God. Who gave you the audacity to even think about these, oh, my children?"

Gold Coast Boy's father expresses his views against biotechnology, genetic engineering, genetically modified organisms or similar technology based on his faith and belief in God. He is aware of biblical references of biotechnology but he does not think any human should mess up with God's creations.

**2.** Mrs. Oleman: "Do not indulge in unnecessary arguments. Do not hangout with gang members. Always carry your bible with you and remember where you come from. Hold high your dignities and those of the Oleman and Nakotey families."

Immigration issues, terrorism around the world including bombings, abductions and shootings in classrooms, churches, mosques, driving vehicles over pedestrians in Africa, USA, and Europe among other places, raises Mrs. Oleman's concerns to the highest level.

**3.** Ibrahim: "You kept your options opened whilst you were chasing your dreams. Here, my true friend, I honor you with my 4 x 200m relay gold medal which is an emblem of oneness, a team, a family, and one world. It also signifies the value of being there for one another, being one another's brother's keeper; one another's sister's keeper."

Ibrahim is a staunch Muslim. Gold Coast Boy is a staunch Christian. The significance of Ibrahim's quotation here using the gold medal he gives to Gold Coast Boy "as an emblem of oneness, a team, a family, and one world" is that Muslims and Christians can work together, can be friends, can form a team and together, they can make the world a peaceful and friendly place for generations upon generations. After all, we are all one race- the human race. We all make mistakes. We are not perfect.

**4.** Gold Coast Boy: "If you dwell on yesterday, you will not know today.

"If you dwell on today, you have no knowledge of yesterday.

"If you dwell on today and yesterday, you are surely going to miss tomorrow.

"Change is inevitable and a necessary event. If you don't change for the better, change will change you and your options will be taken away.

"Innovation springs out of change, knowledge of events and activities of yesterday, today and sticking your neck, heart, soul and mind into tomorrow.

"Yesterday, today and tomorrow. The past, present and the future we cannot live without."

In this quotation and with particular reference to the debate about DNA technology, GMO or biotechnology, Gold Coast Boy points out that to keep the momentum going, one needs to take into account events of the past, present and be courageous enough to face the future. He also highlights innovation which revolves around the desire, willingness and adaptation to change. In so doing, one can continue to find unimaginable solutions to evolving issues of medical interventions, hunger, malnutrition, and the environment that confront humanity.

**5.** In his acceptance speech of the 4 X 200m relay gold medal from his friend Ibrahim, Gold Coast Boy states "This gesture of awarding me with your 4 x 200m relay gold medal will remain golden in my heart forever, Ibrahim. I lack words to express my appreciation to you."

He adds, "And to you all those whose paths I crossed, never forget that you have profoundly impacted the course of my expeditions and reshaped my life in many different ways.

"In the long-run, I hold dear to my heart all the moments we shared together no matter the circumstances throughout the decades of my explorations. You are all assured a special abode in my life."

Here, we see the expression of gratitude from the bottom of his heart to Ibrahim. The forgiveness he freely gives to all those who tried to negatively impact Gold Coast Boy's missions is elegantly and easily voiced out.

As tough as those escapades seem, Gold Coast Boy guarantees the swindlers, fraudsters, those who made fun of him when he suddenly sees himself at the moment of life and death during the gunpoint encounter in the Nigerian military-student rampage and all parties involved, a special place in his heart, just as God forgives us our trespasses.

This recalls what Fatimah once said in the first book, "A Sea of Plight and Pure Joy of the Gold Coast Boy" when she said, "Forgiveness is Noble" which was interpreted by Noble to mean that Fatimah had a crush on him.

Equally, Gold Coast Boy shows his indebtedness to all those who put smiles on his face during his expeditions.

The take-home message is that no matter what the circumstances may be, everyone needs to learn to forgive and to adore one another for peace to prevail on earth. Peace on earth is a shared responsibility.

**6.** "Life is incomplete if it goes without ups and downs", I whispered, and "Without this, we would have viewed our tour from only one angle." Who is making these statements, anyway? (Hint: the author is also a main character in this story).

Life could be boring if it does not throw in the tides going through your spines in your journey's path. Certainly, no tragedies are needed to make life exciting.

**7.** "Burning bridges ignites the flame of global abysmalism beyond factorial quenching proportions."

Here, Nina Willie is urging everyone, not to put an end to opportunities for themselves and for others because you'd never know what may come of tomorrow. She warns that placing stumbling blocks in pursuit of dreams can set the world's menaces, violence, poverty, hatred, chaos, hopelessness and depression on an unstoppable steeple chase.

# INTERPRETATION OF THE AFADJATO CHANT

**1.** Afadjato chant. The Afadjato chant is believed, in this story, to convey the mysteries of the Oleman clan's forefathers in the protection, wisdom, guidance, and the provision of good omen to all descendants of the clan.

# SELECTED FICTION AND NONFICTION

**1.** The creation of the Chimeric biosubmarine is pure fiction and a mystical fantasy.

This seemingly impossible and unimaginative "invention" hopes to expose the youth worldwide to the notion that all things are possible once you put your mind to them.

The reader's attention is drawn to Gold Coast Boy's quotation pertaining to innovation and change in addition to "Yesterday, Today and Sticking your neck and soul into the future."

**2.** While the gunpoint confrontation with the Nigerian military is a true story, the events following this incidence are imaginary. For instance, the activities of Ms. Abbosey and the other parties at the University Hospital are dramatized episodes.

**3.** Multiple drama. CRISPR gene editing is a real promising biotechnology tool. It is critically important to respect rules and regulations when it comes to biotechnology in general as demonstrated in this story by Gold Coast Boy's consultations with regulatory bodies/authorities in the case of Chimeric. Additionally, God did not endow humankind with the ability to be creative by doing things immoral.

In Ghana, the family drama and the Theology of Genetic Engineering Seminary episodes besides the impediments TJ and his daughter Abigail throw in the way of Gold Coast Boy's expeditions are all fiction. And so are the episodes involving the multimedia crew in Nigeria, Ghana and in London.

**4.** The training program in India that Gold Coast Boy and his colleagues undertake is nonfiction. However, the Ama-Gold Coast Boy romantic encounters are purely fiction. Additionally, the trip to the unknown Islands and Sheila's interpretation of the Red Hawk Language are also imaginary. All the events, cities, hotels and tourist attractions in India during the trainees' excursions such as the accidents and near disasters are true spectacles.

**5.** All cities and States (where applicable) in the USA, France and the UK are real but the events have been fictionalized. The WAM entertainment by Nina, the Paris students' get-together involving Le Garcon and the taxi driver are all fiction. The episodes at the Mall of America, Florida Keys, Niagara Falls, Liberty Bell and Tennessee Valley Greyhound Bus terminals, among others, are all fiction.

**6.** The Iowa corn detasseling group and related events are nothing but fiction. The ending of the search for Ibrahim, the circumstances leading to the Drake Relays and the aftermaths of Ibrahim meeting Gold Coast Boy are also tales.

**7.** The Asesewa Biotechnology Center of Excellence is a dream not a real-life facility.

**8.** Tanzania is an East Africa country. However, all scenarios described in this country are tales.

**9.** America's 4th of July party in Ghana: The events described starting from the Grand Canyon to Accra, Akosombo and the Volta Region in Ghana are just fiction.

**10.** The coughing corpse and the cops episode is not a real scenario. It is pure fiction.

**11.** Victoria Falls events and the Search and Find (SAF) five-million-dollar concert aimed at raising awareness about missing and abducted people around the world are purely fictional.

**12.** Undersea battle involving Gold Coast Boy's team and the sharks is fictional.

**13.** Other scenarios are obvious.

# NOTES

# STUDY QUESTIONS AND DISCUSSIONS

**Question 1**

Should the story have ended differently from the way it did? Explain your stand. Sad ending, happy ending, mixed feelings or the story should have been developed further in another book?

**Question 2**

Forgiveness is noble and full of glory. Discuss scenarios where forgiveness has been demonstrated or revealed. Please, be specific.

**Question 3**

Can you describe a time in your life or someone else's life when a person was forgiven? What really happened?

**Question 4**

Some people may make a case for biotechnology or the genetic modification of living organisms by saying that it has done humankind more harm than good. What are your views on this?

**Question 5**

Sometimes, you know a person's "real character" after an unpleasant experience. Where do you see that happen in this story? How did you come to this conclusion?

**Question 6**

The author provided scenarios where empathy has been shown. Please, describe some examples.

**Question 7**

Who are your favorite characters in this story and why?

**Question 8**

Should cultural intelligence be made mandatory in schools and at the work place? Please, address your argument in the form of a letter to a traditional chief in a developing nation or a Chief Executive Officer of a tourist company in the United States.

**Question 9**

If there is any profound lesson that you have learnt in this story, what was it? Please, discuss it.

**Question 10**

What, in your opinion, is the scariest experience in Gold Coast Boy's expeditions? Why is it so?

**Question 11**

What do Mercy and Teye have in common, if any?

**Question 12**

Give an example in your life when you realized that winning or losing is a big responsibility. In other words, accomplishing your dreams or failing to do so is a big responsibility.

**Question 13**

The Gold Coast Boy was faced with series of uncertainties and indecisions at some points in his life. Discuss when you had to make a tough decision in your life. What was the outcome of that decision?

**Question 14**

What was your most memorable childhood friendship experience? Please, share it in your own story book or diary.

**Question 15**

Describe a day you found yourself in a culture different from yours.

**Question 16**

 Family values are crucial to the sustainability of the family. Though tribalism and racism cannot be compared, they all fall under discrimination, a vice that society is still crippled with. Describe a scenario when your friends, family or relatives tried or did in fact put pressure on you because of a person you chose to hang out with? This discussion does not necessarily have to be based on race or tribe only. It can be on religious beliefs, socio-economic status, sexual orientation and/or educational status, among other things.

**Question 17**

In view of Ama's soccer skills and the lesson she teaches the young male soccer players in the Tennessee Valley, should women be encouraged to coach male dominant sports teams? Why or why not?

**Question 18**

Describe four pillars of pure joy of the Gold Coast Boy and two for each of three main characters of your choice.

**Question 19**

What locations in the Gold Coast Boy exploration are the most intriguing to you that you would want to visit before you die? Please describe the specific attractive features.

**Question 20**

Identify and analyze other episodes apart from those described above.

**Question 21**

What are some instances that you would like to share with your friends or book club members that resulted in a search for a lost/ missing or abducted friend, loved one or colleague?

**Question 22**

Your views in the genetic modification of organisms could contribute to the acceptance or rejection of biotechnology in general. Let's hear what your perspectives are.

**Question 23**

Would you give out your hard-won medal or award to a friend whom you believe is a true friend? Why and why not?

**Question 24**

Is it worth your time and risks devoting so much time searching for a lost childhood friend?

**Question 25**

What should Gold Coast Boy have done when two friends Andy and Niifio provide opposing insights into the whereabouts of Ibrahim? Believe in one of them or reject both of them. Why?

**Question 26**

What are some of the most disenchanting tourist sites in Gold Coast Boy's expeditions that you would never like to visit in your life? What is so appalling about these sites?

**Question 27**

Should Gold Coast Boy have gone back home in Africa for an arranged marriage after his explorations?

**Question 28**

What do you make out of the Teye vs Mercy loggerheads? Have you learnt anything from their confrontations?

**Question 29**

What are four of the most challenging obstacles in Gold Coast Boy's expeditions?

**Question 30**

What are some of the most romantic episodes in this story?

**Question 31**

Human beings are to be feared and not Genetic Engineering or Biotechnology. What are your perspectives on this argument?

**Question 32**

Please, enumerate sentences, words or phrases in the book which illustrate or serve as examples for a metaphor, onomatopoeia, simile, personification, hyperbole, rhyme, a symbol or any figure of speech.

NOTES

# SUGGESTED FURTHER READINGS AND SELECTED TRAILS IN THE GOLD COAST BOY EXPEDITION

## INDIA (ASIA)

Ooty in India's Tamil Nadu State. This gorgeous city is embellished with hill resorts, beautiful eucalyptus and pine trees along with other botanical trees and a man-made lake. Retrieved on May 5, 2017 from:

https://www.google.com/search?q=ooty+india&hl=en&auth user=0&source=lnms&tbm=isch&sa=X&ved=0ahUKEwigveC eysvfAhVxm-AKHUgaBwEQ_AUIDygC&cshid=15463113527 89000&biw=512&bih=174&dpr=3.75

**Woodland Hotel** in the city of Chennai (formerly known as Madras until 2000). Chennai is the capital city of Tamil Nadu State, India.

Retrieved on May 5, 2017 from:

https://www.google.com/search?q=Woodland+Hotel+india
&hl=en&authuser=0&sxsrf=ACYBGNSNSxa3xonnnKP8Hxyg
Un5qEiy3IQ:1570541724441&source=lnms&sa=X&ved=0ah
UKEwiHhdzs44zlAhUpmuAKHUu2DaMQ_AUIDCgA&biw=54
4&bih=209&dpr=3.53

**Savera Hotel** in the city of Chennai (formerly known as Madras until 2000). Chennai is the capital city of Tamil Nadu State, India.

Retrieved on May 5, 2017 from:

https://www.google.com/search?hl=en&authuser=0&biw=5
44&bih=209&tbm=isch&sxsrf=ACYBGNRqNiNhwbXLtmEqw
xeZHfl80POn5A%3A1570543107180&sa=1&ei=A5acXc7QC
qOyggesrLKQBQ&q=Savera+Hotel+india&oq=Savera+Hot
el+india&gs_l=img.3...0.0..8255...0.0..0.0.0.......0......gws-wiz-
img.C7k9gs8mpnY&ved=0ahUKEwiO3oeA6YzlAhUjmeAKH
SyWDFIQ4dUDCAY&uact=5

**Tamil Nadu Agricultural University** in Tamil Nadu, India.

Retrieved on May 5, 2017 from:

https://www.google.com/search?hl=en&authuser=0&biw=5
12&bih=174&tbm=isch&sa=1&ei=O9kqXP-yKNHn_Qb2xbq
ABQ&q=Tamil+Nadu+Agricultural+University+india&oq=Ta
mil+Nadu+Agricultural+University+india&gs_l=img.3..0i24.1
96078.201424..207411...0.0..0.59.759.15......0....1j2..gws-wiz-
img.......0j0i67.yH4tu_dLH-g))

**Coimbatore** (also known as Koval) is a major city in Tamil Nadu State, India.

Retrieved on May 5, 2017 from:

https://www.google.com/search?hl=en&authuser=0&biw
=512&bih=174&tbm=isch&sa=1&ei=C9oqXPeEKO6L_Qb
5ubTwBQ&q=Coimbatore+india&oq=Coimbatore+india&
gs_l=img.3..0l2j0i7i30l5j0i7i5i30l2j0i8i30.157392.160519..
163571...0.0..0.65.1737.35......0....1j2..gws-wiz-img.......0i67.
N0OFRzUkA5Q

**Nilgiri hills** form part of the mountain ranges called the Ghats. Also known as the Nigiri Mountains, they are in Tamil Nadu State but spread over parts of Kerala and Karnataka States.

Retrieved on May 5, 2017 from:

https://www.google.com/search?q=nilgiri+hills&source=lnm
s&tbm=isch&sa=X&ved=0ahUKEwiXuuGc2MvfAhWCVN8KH
Td8ClYQ_AUIDigB&cshid=1546315079631000&biw=512&
bih=174

**Central Food Technological Research Institute** is a prominent institution of learning in Mysore located in the State of Karnataka. Mysore is also known for its rich historic cultural centers. The Mysore Zoo is a major center of attraction.

Retrieved on May 5, 2017 from:

https://www.google.com/search?q=Central+Food+Tech
nological+Research+Institute&source=lnms&tbm=isch&
sa=X&ved=0ahUKEwi73aDY2svfAhXNY98KHV93AcsQ_
AUIECgD&biw=512&bih=174

**Maharaja's Palace** in Mysore, Karnataka State in India. It boasts
of one of the must-see historic places in India.

Retrieved on May 5, 2017 from:

https://www.google.com/search?q=maharaja's+palace&tbm
=isch&source=univ&sa=X&ved=2ahUKEwiLpvXRsoflAhUFvF
kKHa2YAwsQsAR6BAgGEAE&biw=427&bih=143&dpr=4.5

**Hotel Harsha** in the city of Hyderabad in Andhra Pradesh State
of India. Retrieved on May 5, 2017 from:

https://www.google.com/search?q=hotel+Harsha&source=ln
ms&tbm=isch&sa=X&ved=0ahUKEwiBqLWe5MvfAhXuYt8KH
eD7CHsQ_AUIDygC&biw=512&bih=174

**Scientific and Technological Museum** in Bangalore in the
Indian State of Karnataka. Places of interest in Bangalore include
the aquarium, botanical garden and Central Library.

Retrieved on May 5, 2017 from:

https://www.google.com/search?biw=512&bih=174&tbm=i
sch&sa=1&ei=T-sqXMnTFual_QbfyKrABw&q=Scientific+and
+Technological+Museum+in+Bangalore&oq=Scientific+an
d+Technological+Museum+in+Bangalore&gs_l=img.3...296
560.296560..316402...0.0..0.51.51.1......0....1j2..gws-wiz-img.
aQ3rQ8-Jlpo

**Majesty Cine Mall**, located in the Madurai District of Tamil Nadu
State in India.

Retrieved on May 5, 2017 from:

https://www.google.com/search?q=Majesty+Cine+Mall,+in+
INDIA&source=lnms&tbm=isch&sa=X&ved=0ahUKEwjQwtv
osdjeAhUOpFkKHeqDBz0Q_AUIDygC&biw=853&bih=290

**United Kingdom (UK)-London (EUROPE)**

Trafalgar Square, London in the United Kingdom (UK). This popular center of attraction has a rich historic story to tell besides
the pigeons. Retrieved on May 5, 2017 from:

https://www.google.com/search?biw=512&bih=174&tbm=is
ch&sa=1&ei=k_EqXL3jG6uOggfOkZP4Dg&q=trafalgar+squ
are+london&oq=Trafalgar+Square&gs_l=img.1.3.0j0i67j0l8.
916699.924607..932161...0.0..0.57.205.4......0....1j2..gws-wiz-
img.INfbOYGI8-A

**FRANCE-Paris (EUROPE)**

**Eiffel Tower** in Paris. Is a popular French historic site.

Retrieved on May 5, 2017 from:

https://www.google.com/search?q=Eiffel+Tower&source=ln ms&tbm=isch&sa=X&ved=0ahUKEwiMzonC6cvfAhUSneAKH d8PBa0Q_AUIDigB&biw=512&bih=174

**UNITED STATES OF AMERICA -USA- (NORTH AMERICA)**

**1. Grand Canyon:** This spectacular 1 mile (1.61 kilometers) deep  Grand Canyon tourist site in Arizona attracts about 5.5 million people every year, offers a lot to see and to enrich your knowledge.

Retrieved on July 4, 2018 from:

https://www.nps.gov/inde/learn/historyculture/stories-liber-tybell.htm

and from:

https://www.google.com/search?hl=en&authuser=0&biw=5 12&bih=174&tbm=isch&sa=1&ei=TtxKXNzWCe3s_Qaq6ZL wDQ&q=grand+canyon&oq=grand+canyon&gs_l=img.3.0 .0l10.333654.340314..370100...0.0..0.158.950.9j3......0....1.. gws-wizimg.......0i67.CkUM9by7p_0

**2. Hoover Dam:** "Hoover Dam stores water that irrigates 2 million acres, not only in the rich farm fields of Southern California's Imperial Valley, but across the state line in Arizona. Hoover Dam generates enough hydroelectric power to serve 1.3 million people each year, provides municipal water for urban centers including Los Angeles, Phoenix and Tucson, holds back flood waters, provides storage during drought and takes more than a little credit for the unabashed growth of the desert Southwest".

Retrieved on July 4, 2018 from:

https://www.nps.gov/articles/nevada-and-arizona-hoover-dam.htm

and from:

https://www.google.com/search?q=hoover+dam&hl=en&authuser=0&source=lnms&tbm=isch&sa=X&sqi=2&ved=0ahUKEwj4852gw7LgAhWOKlAKHY8tA0EQ_AUIDygC&biw=512&bih=174

**3. Mall of America, Minnesota.** This mall in the Minneapolis suburb of Bloomington is one of a kind with lots of fun, shopping, dining and more. It is America's biggest mall.

Retrieved on July 4, 2018 from:

https://www.google.com/search?q=Mall+of+America&source=lnms&tbm=isch&sa=X&ved=0ahUKEwjOjtbg0NPfAhWNVN8KHeEpDQYQ_AUIECgD&biw=512&bih=174

**4. Liberty Bell**, Philadelphia, Pennsylvania. Is one of America's most significant historical sites you should not miss if and when you visit the United States.

Retrieved on July 4, 2018 from:

https://www.google.com/search?q=liberty+bell&hl= en&authuser=0&source=lnms&tbm=isch&sa=X&sqi= 2&ved=0ahUKEwiphaPU09PfAhUFQZAKHWGjA5sQ_ AUIDigB&biw=512&bih=174

'The Liberty Bell' bears a timeless message: "Proclaim Liberty Throughout All the Land Unto All the Inhabitants thereof". "Go beyond the iconic crack to learn how this State House bell was transformed into an extraordinary symbol. Abolitionists, women's suffrage advocates and Civil Rights leaders took inspiration from the inscription on this bell". Retrieved on July 4, 2018 from: https://www.nps.gov/inde/learn/historyculture/stories-liberty-bell.htm

**5. Florida Keys** in the State of Florida. Learn about the fascinating history of the Florida Keys including several bridges connecting the islands.

Retrieved on July 4, 2018 from:

https://www.google.com/search?q=florida+keys& hl=en&authuser=0&source=lnms&tbm=isch&sa=X &ved=0ahUKEwie59_m1tPfAhUrmuAKHdfZD-0Q_ AUIDygC&biw=512&bih=174

**6. The Drake Relays,** Des Moines, Iowa. Started in 1910 and twelve years later, it became the first major track and field event to be on radio broadcast.

Retrieved on July 4, 2018 from:

https://www.google.com/search?q=drake+relays&hl=en&aut huser=0&source=lnms&tbm=isch&sa=X&ved=0ahUKEwjo85 u82NPfAhXvmeAKHStlCaMQ_AUIECgD&biw=512&bih=174

**7. Corn detasseling.** Manual corn detasseling is a symbol of industriousness. If you have not done manual corn detasseling in the Iowa corn fields under extreme weather conditions, you may not know what hard labor really means.

**NIGERIA (AFRICA)**

**Ahmadu Bello University (ABU),** Zaria, Nigeria. ABU was established in 1962 shortly after Nigeria's independence from British colonial rule in 1960. It is one of the most prominent universities in Nigeria in addition to the first university in the nation, University of Ibadan which was established in 1948.

Retrieved on February 22, 2017 from:

https://www.google.com/search?q=ahmadu+bello+univer sity+zaria+nigeria&hl=en&authuser=0&source=lnms&tbm =isch&sa=X&ved=0ahUKEwiQ15Hw3tPfAhUlUt8KHephBj 8Q_AUIECgD&biw=512&bih=174

## GHANA (AFRICA)

**Akosombo Dam** This hydroelectric dam at Akosombo in Ghana is not only a major source of electricity supply in Ghana and some of the neighboring countries but a major tourist site in the country.

Retrieved on February 22, 2017 from:

https://www.google.com/search?q=akosombo+da
m&hl=en&authuser=0&source=lnms&tbm=isch&sa
=X&ved=0ahUKEwj23pfry4jgAhVShuAKHRkuAr4Q_
AUIDygC&biw=512&bih=174

**Boti Water Falls** Is located in a quiet village called Boti in the Manya Krobo district of the Eastern Region in Ghana and not far from Asesewa. The Boti Falls is an amazing waterfall which is embedded at the heart of the forest reserve in the town of Huhunya, which is found about 17km North-East of Koforidua, the regional capital.

Retrieved on February 22, 2017 from:

https://www.google.com/search?q=boti+falls+ghana&
hl=en&authuser=0&source=lnms&tbm=isch&sa=X&sq
i=2&ved=0ahUKEwiN5OWXstjeAhWstlkKHXkaCrcQ_
AUIDygC&biw=853&bih=290

and from:

https://www.modernghana.com/news/649593/boti-falls-not-just-water.html

**Mountain Afadjato** is the highest mountain in Ghana and stands at an altitude of 885m(2,905ft). The mountain is located in the Agmatsa Range and runs along the Ghana-Togo border near the village of Liati Wote and Gbledi.

Retrieved on August 18, 2018 from:

https://www.google.com/search?q=mt+afadjato+ghana&hl=en&authuser=0&-source=lnms&tbm=isch&sa=X&sqi=2&ved=0ahUKEwjfy5vBstjeAh-WrtlkKHVTlA-IQ_AUIDygC&biw=853&bih=290

and from:

http://amedzofevillage.com/en/2016/04/21/mt-afadjato/

"Mount Afadjato on a clear day, offers views of the neighboring villages, the Tagbo waterfalls, and the Volta Lake. From the peak, visitors can enjoy fantastic panoramic views of surrounding villages, forests, mountains, valleys and Volta Lake which are all visible from the summit".

**Volta Lake** (or Lake Volta) is a man-made lake in Ghana built on the Akosombo Dam and generates electricity to the country and some of its neighbors.

Retrieved on February 22, 2017 from:

https://www.britannica.com/place/Lake-Volta

and from:

https://www.google.com/search?q=volta+lake+in+gh
ana&hl=en&authuser=0&source=lnms&tbm=isch&sa
=X&ved=0ahUKEwi2rrC_1ljgAhUOWN8KHRHrCl4Q_
AUIDigB&biw=512&bih=174

**Movenpick Ambassador Hotel**

Is a Five-Star hotel formerly known as the Ambassador Hotel.

Retrieved on February 22, 2017 from:

https://www.movenpick.com/en/africa/ghana/accra/
moevenpick-ambassador-hotel-accra/overview/

and from:

https://www.google.com/search?q=movenpick+accra&r
lz=1C1SQJL_enUS796US796&source=lnms&tbm=isch&
sa=X&ved=0ahUKEwjf6ImhpK3gAhXpguAKHUzFAeYQ_
AUIDygC&biw=512&bih=174

**Kempinski Hotel**

This ultramodern Five-Star Hotel in Accra is a popular spot for vacationers and travelers.

Retrieved on February 22, 2017 from:

https://www.google.com/search?q=kempinski+hotel+accr
a&rlz=1C1SQJL_enUS796US796&source=lnms&tbm=isch
&sa=X&ved=0ahUKEwi325i5pa3gAhUITt8KHTbCCmoQ_
AUIDygC&biw=512&bih=174

and from:

https://www.kempinski.com/en/accra/hotel-gold-coast-city/

**TANZANIA (AFRICA)**

**Mount Kilimanjaro**

Mount Kilimanjaro, located in the Eastern African country of
Tanzania is the highest mountain on the continent of Africa with
an elevation of 19,341 ft (5,895 meters) above sea level. It is a
very popular attraction for travelers and mountain climbers from
around the world.

Retrieved on September 7, 2018 from:

https://www.google.com/search?q=mount+kilimanjaro
&hl=en&authuser=0&source=lnms&tbm=isch&sa=X&sq
i=2&ved=0ahUKEwj07JqbxYjgAhVKOK0KHXvGBCEQ_
AUIDigB&biw=512&bih=174

## ZIMBABWE (AFRICA)

Victoria Falls' elegance is splendidly displayed on Africa's fourth largest river, River Zambezi in the Republic of Zimbabwe. The country boasts not only of its Victoria Falls which is considered to be the largest River Fall in the world but also ranks as a superior site of attraction in Africa which magnetizes travelers from all corners of the universe. Victoria Falls' soothing sound from the mist is not viewed just a relaxation therapy but a soul and heart cooling experience that can last forever.

Retrieved on April 11, 2018 from:

https://victoriafallstourism.org/

and

https://www.google.com/search?q=victoria+fall s+zimbabwe&source=lnms&tbm=isch&sa=X&ve d=0ahUKEwjhmq3I4cjhAhXszVkKHWUoABYQ_ AUIDygC&biw=571&bih=188&dpr=3.3

## Other References

## CRISPR/cas9 gene editing

Retrieved on August 20, 2016 from

https://www.synthego.com/resources/crispr-101-ebook?utm_term=what%20is%20crispr%20cas9&utm_campaign=2018-06+CRISPR+General&utm_source=adwords&utm_medium=ppc&hsa_tgt=kwd-344750348768&hsa_grp=56222315276&hsa_src=g&hsa_net=adwords&hsa_mt=e&hsa_ver=3&hsa_ad=277181102876&hsa_acc=6964378581&hsa_kw=what%20is%20crispr%20cas9&hsa_cam=1433665177&gclid=EAIaIQobChMIoJzSpu_c3wIVB-h3Ch3Q0gt3EAAYAiAAEgIb8PD_BwE

**CRISPR gene editing**

Retrieved on August 20, 2018 from

https://gs.harvardx.harvard.edu/harvard-crispr-gene-editing-applications-online-short-course-sf/?ef_id=c%3A318503670122_d%3Ac_n%3Ag_ti%3Akwd-317599818853_p%3A_k%3A%2Bcrispr_m%3Ab_a%3A62703010079&gclid=EAIaIQobChMInYmF4PDc3wIVkZ-fCh0e2A70EAAYASAAEgJ6xvD_BwE

**Gene replacement therapy**

Retrieved on August 20, 2018 from

https://www.exploregenetherapy.com/?utm_
source=ppc&utm_medium=online&utm_campaign=pep-
unbranded-unbranded-search-032018&utm_
content=consumer-patient-genetic-disorders-101&gc
lid=EAIaIQobChMI8pe64fHc3wIVk4TICh13BQq_
EAAYBCAAEgJqNvD_BwE

**Africa, the youngest continent**

Retrieved on August 20, 2018 from

https://www.un.org/sustainabledevelopment/blog/2017/10/
with-fast-growing-youth-population-africa-boasts-enormous-
market-potential-un-deputy-chief/

**World population prospects**

Retrieved on August 20, 2018 from

https://www.un.org/development/desa/en/news/population/
world-population-prospects-2017.html

# ACKNOWLEDGEMENT

The late Mr. Philip Stinard is greatly and sincerely appreciated for devoting his precious time in reviewing the manuscript and making valuable suggestions prior to his passing away.

www.ingramcontent.com/pod-product-compliance
Lightning Source LLC
Chambersburg PA
CBHW051313170626
46809CB00004B/1876